How the
CAMEL
Got His Hump

For Hannah, Imogen and William

Find out more about

Rudyard Kipling's JUST SO STORIES

at Shoo Rayner's fabulous website,

www.shoo-rayner.co.uk

First published in 2007 by Orchard Books
First paperback publication in 2008

ORCHARD BOOKS
338 Euston Road, London NW1 3BH
Orchard Books Australia
Level 17/207 Kent St, Sydney, NSW 2000

ISBN 978 1 84616 398 2 (hardback)
ISBN 978 1 84616 407 1 (paperback)

A CIP catalogue record for this book is available from the British Library.

1 3 5 7 9 10 8 6 4 2 (hardback)
1 3 5 7 9 10 8 6 4 2 (paperback)

Printed and bound in China by Imago

Orchard Books is a division of Hachette Children's Books,
an Hachette Livre UK company.

www.orchardbooks.co.uk

Rudyard Kipling's
JUST SO STORIES

How the
CAMEL
Got His Hump

Retold and illustrated by
SHOO RAYNER

ORCHARD BOOKS

Long, long ago, at the very beginning of time, when everything was just getting sorted out, and the Animals were just beginning to work for Man, there was a Camel.

The Camel had a long neck and long legs and a long straight back, that he was very proud of.

Because he did not want to work and bend his back, the Camel lived in the middle of a Howling Desert, where he ate sticks and thorns and tamarisks and milkweed and prickles.

Things to eat in a Howling Desert

Sticks
Dry but very filling.

Thorns
Quite a sharp flavour.

Tamarisks
Delicate and feathery, but insubstantial.

Milkweed
Tastes a bit like cheese.

Prickles
Mouthwateringly painful!

The Camel was most excruciatingly idle. When anybody spoke to him he said, "Humph!" Just "Humph!" And that was all he said.

On Monday morning, the Horse came
to see him. The Horse had a saddle on
his back and a halter on his head.

11

He called to the
Camel, "Camel, oh
Camel, come out
and trot like the
rest of us."

"Humph!"

"Humph!"
said the Camel.
And that was
all he said.

12

The Horse trotted away and
told the Man what had happened.

A little while later, the Dog came along. The Dog had a stick in his mouth. The Dog called to the Camel, "Camel, oh Camel, come and fetch and carry like the rest of us."

"Humph!"

"Humph!" said the Camel. And that was all he said.

The Dog went away and told
the Man what had happened.

Not long after, the Ox came to see the Camel. The Ox had a yoke on his neck. "Camel, oh Camel," the Ox bellowed. "Come and plough the fields like the rest of us."

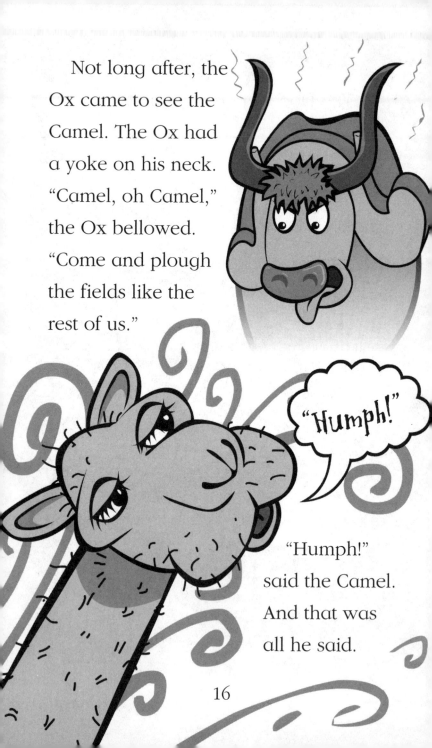

"Humph!"

"Humph!" said the Camel. And that was all he said.

The Ox went away and told
the Man what had happened.

At the end of the day the Man
called the Horse and the Dog and the
Ox together.

"I'm very sorry, you three," he said, "but that Humph-thing in the Howling Desert can't do any work. If he could, he would. I am going to leave him alone, and you will have to work double-time to make up for him."

That made the Horse and the Dog and the Ox very angry. They held a powwow on the edge of the Howling Desert.

The Camel watched them, while chewing milkweed in a most excruciatingly idle way. Then he laughed at the three friends, said, "Humph!" and went away into the desert again.

Excruciatingly Idle Creatures

The slimy, sleepy, somnolent sloth is so slow that mould grows on its fur.

The koala sleeps in the eucalyptus tree for twenty-two hours a day. It wakes up only to reach out and eat a leaf.

The stick insect acts as if it's stuck!

The spider sits around all day waiting for dinner to serve itself.

Back in those days, there were Jinns and Angels and other kinds of spirits, who were in charge of getting the world sorted out.

The Jinn in charge of All the Deserts came howling along in a cloud of dust. He stopped for a chat with the three friends.

24

Jinns

Jinns are different
from angels.
Angels have wings.

A jinn is not a genie.
Genies live in lamps and
other small dark places.

Jinns are not spirits.
Spirits float in strange,
wispy ways.

You will only know what a jinn
is when you meet one.

"Jinn of All the Deserts," the Horse asked. "Is it right for anyone to be idle – what with everything only just getting sorted out and all?"

"Certainly not!" said the Jinn.

"Well," said the Horse, "there's a thing in the middle of your Howling Desert, with a long neck and long legs and a long straight back. He hasn't done a stroke of work since Monday morning. He won't even trot."

"Well!" said the Jinn, whistling like the desert wind. "That'll be my Camel! What does he have to say about it?"

"He says 'Humph!'" the Dog whined.

"He won't fetch or carry either."

"Does he say anything else?" asked the Jinn.

"Only 'Humph!'" moaned the Ox. "And he won't even plough the fields."

The Jinn tapped the
side of his nose. "Leave
it to me," he said. "I'll
give him humph!"

The Jinn wrapped himself up in his dust-cloak, and swept through the Howling Desert. He found the Camel in an oasis. He was being most excruciatingly idle, staring at his own reflection in a pool of water.

"My grumpy old friend," said the Jinn.
"I hear you've not been working."

"Humph!" said the Camel.

The Jinn sat down, with his chin in
his hand and thought. The Camel
continued staring at his reflection.

"Because of your excruciating idleness," said the Jinn, "you've given the Horse and the Dog and the Ox extra work ever since Monday morning."

"Humph!" said the Camel.

"I shouldn't say that again if I were you," the Jinn warned. "You might say it once too often. I want you to get to work right now!"

And the Camel said "Humph!" again.
But no sooner had he said it than the
Camel's long straight back, that he was
so proud of, puffed up and up, into a
great, big, lolloping humph.

"There!" said the Jinn. "That's your very own humph that you've brought upon yourself by not working. Today is Thursday, and you've not worked since Monday. You will have to work hard to catch up."

"How can I work with this humph on my back?" the Camel grumbled.

"That humph is made for a purpose," the Jinn explained. "You can live off your humph. It will let you work for three days without eating.

"Now, come out of
the Howling Desert
and behave – and
humph yourself!"

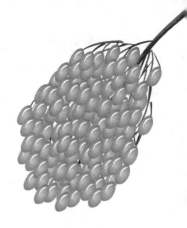

The Camel humphed himself, humph and all, and went away to join the Horse and the Dog and the Ox.

Humphs and Humps

"Humph!"

"Humph!"

We all get a bit like the camel,
When we feel down and blue.

Yes, we all get like the camel then,
But he knows just what to do.

Get out in the howling desert,
And walk for mile upon mile.

Then that awful humph you're feeling,
Will turn into a wide happy smile!

From that day on, the Camel has always worn a humph (except we call it a "hump" now, so as not to hurt his feelings).

But the Camel has never caught up with the three days that he missed at the very beginning of time, when everything was just getting sorted out. And, he has never yet learned how to behave!

"Humph!"

Rudyard Kipling's JUST SO STORIES

Retold and illustrated by
SHOO RAYNER

All priced at £3.99

Rudyard Kipling's Just So Stories are available from all good bookshops,
or can be ordered direct from
the publisher: Orchard Books, PO BOX 29, Douglas IM99 1BQ
Credit card orders please telephone 01624 836000
or fax 01624 837033 or visit our internet site: www.orchardbooks.co.uk
or e-mail: bookshop@enterprise.net for details.

To order please quote title, author and ISBN
and your full name and address.
Cheques and postal orders should be made payable to 'Bookpost plc.'
Postage and packing is FREE within the UK
(overseas customers should add £2.00 per book).

Prices and availability are subject to change.